First published in Great Britain by Kindle Direct Publishing

Copyright © Dini Armstrong and Sarah Armstrong 2021

All illustrations are created by Sarah Armstrong (Fitzblocksberg Illustrations)

The right of Dini Armstrong to be identified as the Author of the Work has been asserted by her in accordance with the Copyright, Designs and Patents Act 1988.

All rights reserved. No parts of this publication might be reproduced, stored in a retrieval system or transmitted, in any form or by any means, without the prior written permission of Dini Armstrong and Sarah Armstrong, nor be otherwise circulated in any form of binding or cover other than that in which it is published and without a similar condition being imposed on the subsequent purchaser.

KDP ISBN: 9798476081555

www.DiniArmstrong.com

www.Fitzblocksberg.com

Ghosts in the Toolbox

and other nonsense

Dini Armstrong

and

Sarah Armstrong

The Trap

My mother shoves a piece of carrot cake aside and adds a scone to my plate, already filled with clotted cream and jam, before reaching for pie.
'How many slices would you like?' 'I'm fine,' I try but my resistance crumbles. She pinches my left cheek and tuts.
'You're getting chubby, girl!'

Unvanquished

Ma wife's a belter. Wee bit blootered mebbie, skirt pure short under cap'n gown, still fits an all. Creepin' Jesus winkin' at her.
Auldjins on stage are struttin' in foosty suits, peely wally wi' the strain of it.
That's her name noo.
'Da, is that you bawlin'?'
'Haud yer wheesht.'

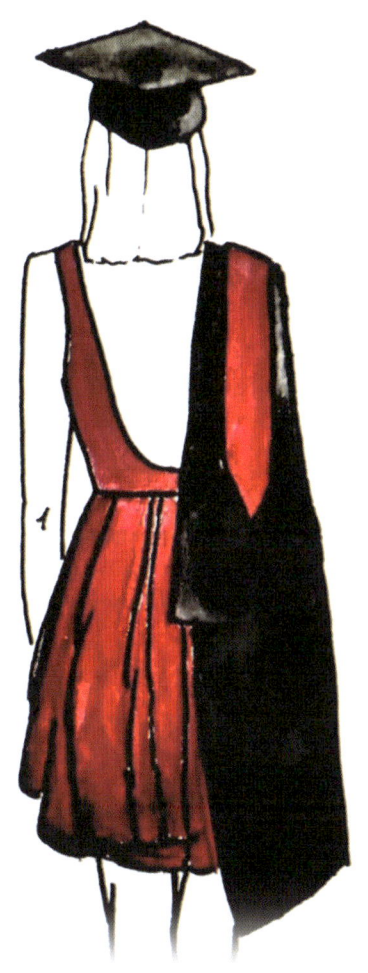

Little Lion

The lion's sad, he is wretched, woebegone and glum. He mopes and hangs his head; his mighty mane, once tall and proud, is hanging lower still. The tail is dragging on the ground. What happened here, my friend? There's ham, I saw, I smelled. But then she went and closed the fridge.

Pirates

This buccaneer prefers the crow's nest to the berth, despite a surging storm. With shivering timbers, aye, we will prevail, our skull and bones won't break! A few weeks more, and yellow fever notwithstanding, the treasure will be ours.
"Come on, my girl, it's time for tea!"
"Oh mum, five minutes more!"

Derailed

Club 27 passed me by, now it's Club 50 Scotrail card. Grey hair, soft flesh and comfy pants are playing hide and seek, and yet I hear them giggle.
Conductor guy exclaims that I don't look my age, and I am lost for words, offended by my smile. How can I not?

Birth/Death

Four women gather round a bed to help a fifth. She's lying there in agony, her stomach swollen and her breathing shallow.
'Not long now,' they promise her, 'it's over soon.' Their eyes full of love, their chests are filled with doubt. Dawn gives way to dusk with no rest in between.

The Very Profound Poem

Inside a dusty box, I found a poem,
written by my younger self, addressed to him,
my soul mate, source of agony and bliss.
Fuelled by visceral accounts of our passion and his
perfidy I was determined I would never love again.
If only I could remember who I wrote this for.

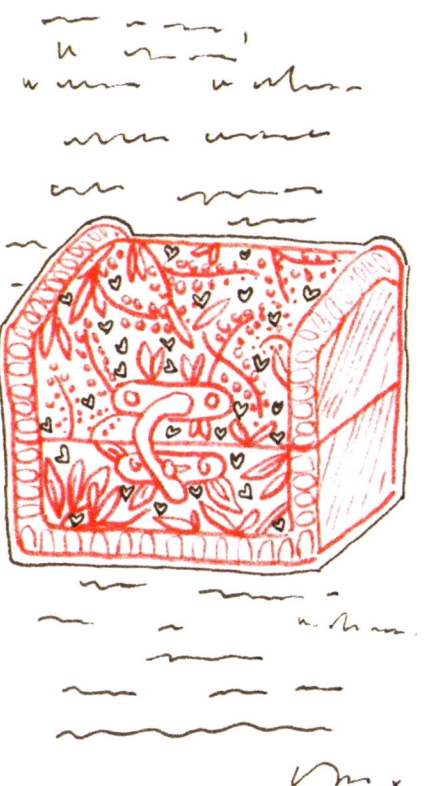

Bottled Up

'You're a bit hard to swallow sometimes,' he says, so she bottles it all up and keeps a lid on it, before retreating to the highest shelf. She clutches her chest and commits her thoughts to paper. Maybe she has to cast herself away before the message can be found and reassembled.

The astute cat

My cat cannot be fooled with 'Nothing, I'm just tired.' She will insist on lying on my lap, purring me into admission. I am not okay.
I need that cuddle more than you will know.
'Maybe just go to bed a little earlier tonight,' my husband offers.
I nod and smile.

Counterfeit Pennies

It's her birthday, but something is missing.
A white hole in her chest, she paints another
woman's face onto her own – it's not enough.
She dresses for her party, rehearses selfie
smirks – they look offbeat.
One of these days she'll find a penny on the
ground and walk right past.

A predator in the field

I hesitate. Will it be safe to cross? I look at her. Hey, you, I shout, is there much danger here? Still masticating, she musters me, her eyes are soft and brown, framed with thick lashes, a gentle giant.
Oh yes, she nods, the danger lies in you. You kill.

Thirty Birthday Cakes

You've been my son for thirty years, and I have been your mum. You learned to walk, to speak, to play alone.
I learned to grow a child, to birth, to bathe, to feed, to kiss a knee in pain. We both helped raise each other, we both learned how to live.

The Hotel Lift

Beads of sweat are forming on Lisa's forehead. All that garlic, not a great choice with IBS. With gas bubbles ramming her sphincter, she moves to the back of the lift. Clench buttocks, think of…rabbits knitting hats, splashing in puddles, folding sheets! Nope, too late.
Oh god, we're sharing rooms tonight.

A Kiss on Quicksand

We sat on swings, beside each other, moving from left to right so that our hands would touch, beneath us playground sand.
I pressed my face against the cold and rusty chain. You leaned towards me and your lips touched mine. It threw us both off balance, that first kiss.

Elizabeth Hopkins did not cry

Witnesses claimed the eight-year-old's petticoats had been removed, the accused was indeed lying on top of her. Doctors confirmed her shamefully abused, with injury sustained. 'Impossible!' cried members of the Jury. 'A child so young cannot be ravished, and we know she did not cry!'
The rapist did. He hanged.

(Based on the real-life trial of Stephen Arrowsmith, as described in the archives of the Old Bailey, trial date 11th September 1678.)

The New World starts at Ten

I was ten when the world changed.
The ugly beige wallpaper at the optician's was suddenly revealed as a medieval landscape, complete with jousting knights, dragons, castles and princesses.
'So?' asked the optometrist.
'That's great,' I said. But deep inside lingered a sad little question:
'What else have I missed?

Itching

Just itching to escape this dive, I'll find another club. We'll ride the Black Eagle together, friend, we'll soar towards the flickering and bright. My mama always said aim high. Here's just the tingle first, and then the prick: Oh yes, and YES and FUCKING SCORE!
We'll dive and crash alone.

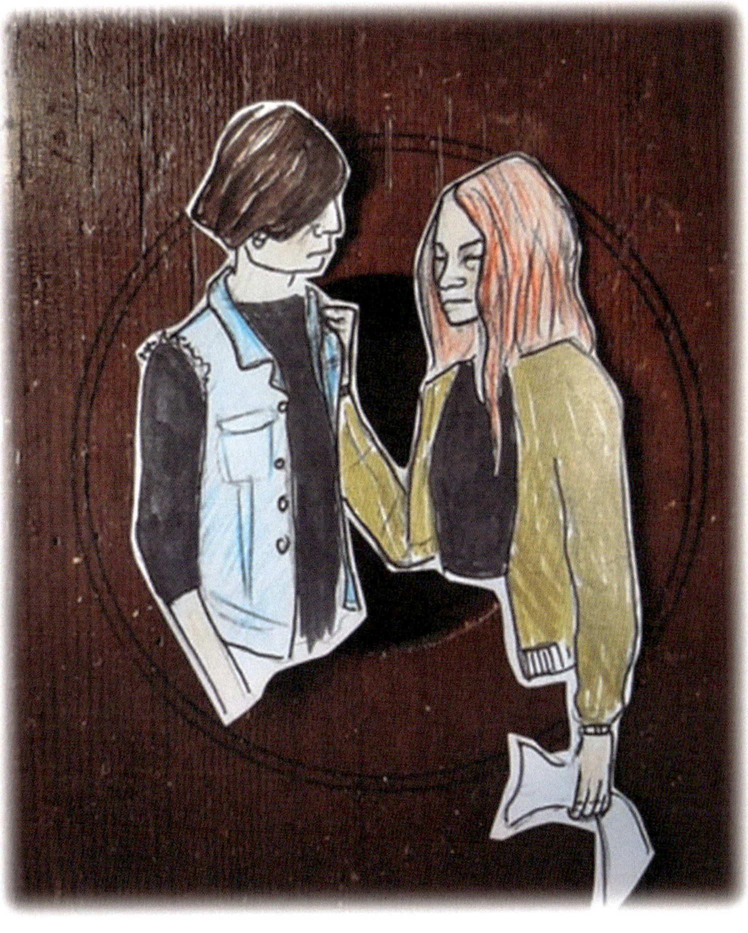

Khaleesi's Gift

The wise man will be reading from the scroll –
and you'll be liberated from the pain of loss
and insignificance. Received with zeal, the
dragon will be yours, the rhythm of his sway
betray his adoration. A great escape, my
queen,
the day when you'll inherit
that pet lizard from your aunt.

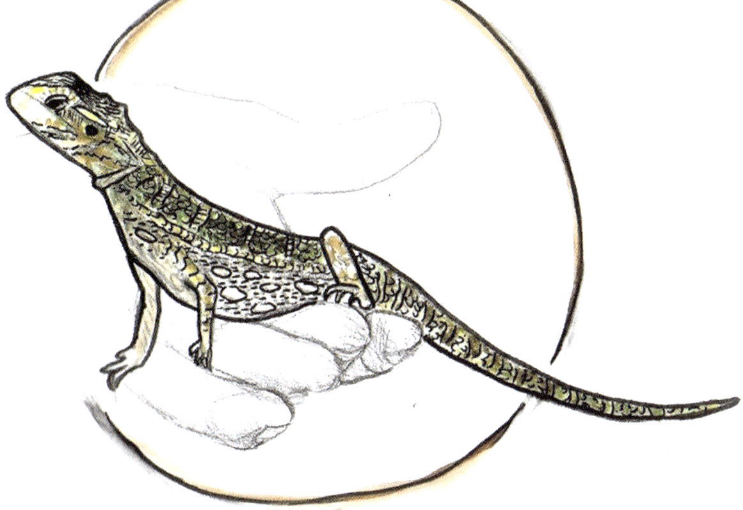

Extra-terrestrial Crisis

I sensed impending doom before the orbital spacecraft was even launched. I knew for sure when the first team member of the dramatic exploration mission declared: 'We have visual on Mars,' his ship already dwarfed by the red planet. It was true. There were no decent SciFis left on Netflix.

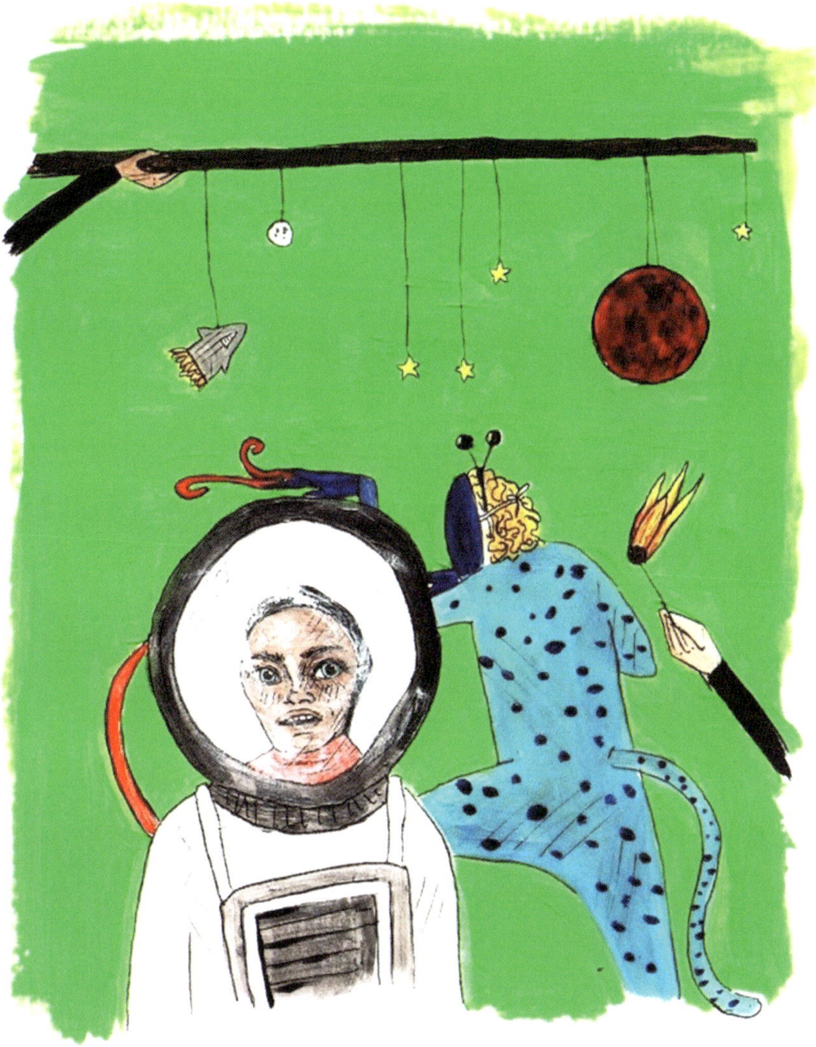

The Miracle

On Friday, not so Good for him, a bunny, dipped in molten chocolate, was buried in a sheath of silver foil. His body was displayed for all to see and guarded heavily. And yet, in Sunday's morning light, when cleaning women came to see, they found it gone. Nothing but empty shelves.

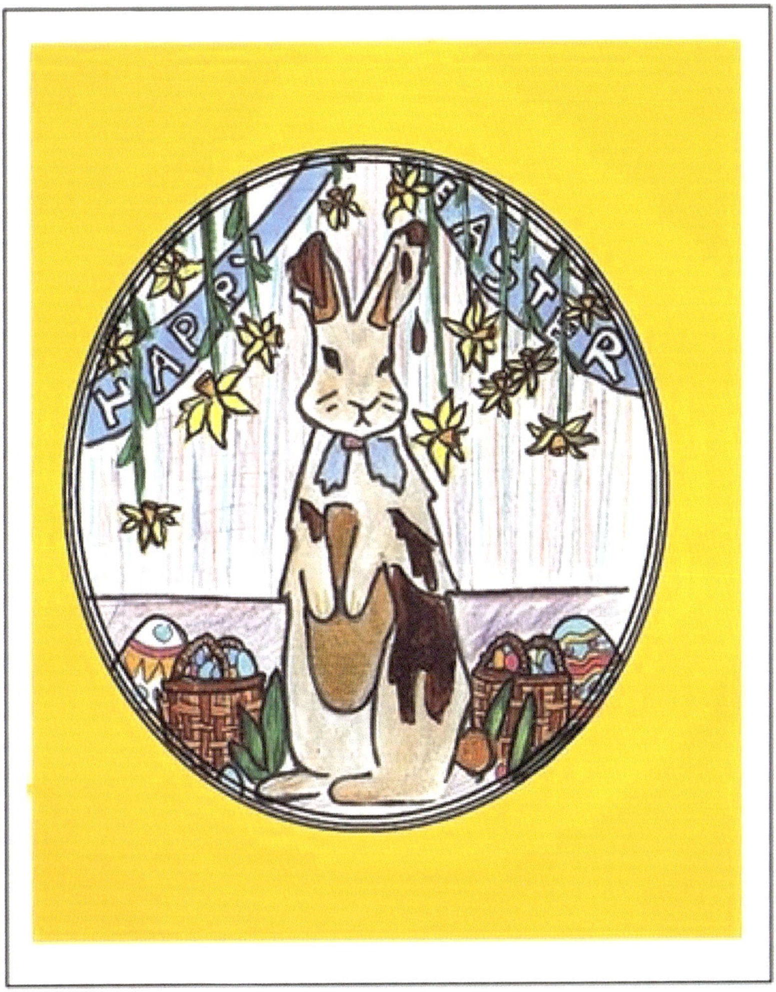
HAPPY EASTER

Lynched

The girl looked pale, she let out a scream that chilled us to the core. Her mother ran to her attention, searched for the cause, but not a scratch. And then they turned to me, the single stranger, next to her, alone.
But no one saw – the ice cream on the floor.

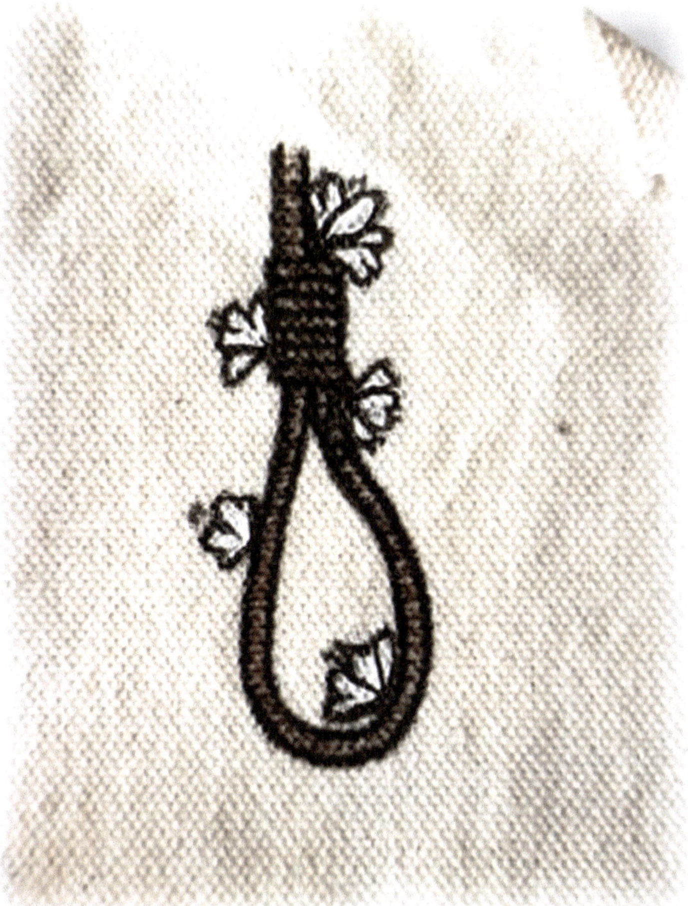

Psilocybe semilanceata

A glorious day in the forest,
foraging in fresh air, kids, who needs supermarkets?
Try a nibble of this delicious mushroom, we'll fry that with butter at home. Who finds most berries? Oh, that fluffy ray of light is just so beautiful, come stroke this tree.
Wait, are those badgers playing trumpets?

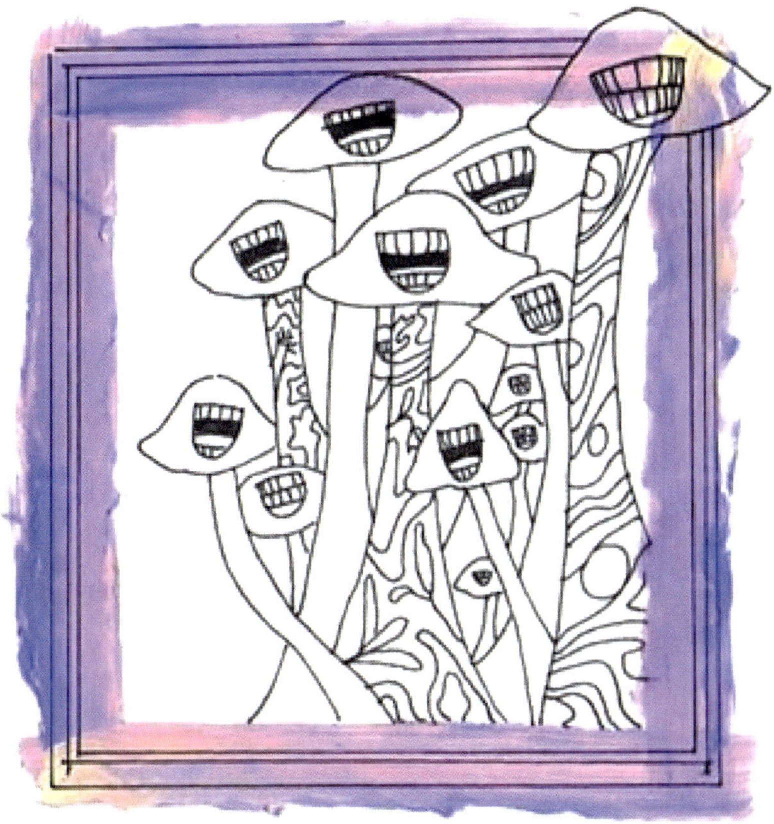

Clobbered with a pee stick

Arguing in a cold one-bedroom, muffled screams under pillows. Clobbering promotions with a pee stick and two stripes. Mopping up coffee you've just spilled in a cold wet country whilst your other half buggered off on holiday to Spain. Mopping up blood in a hot dry country – seems easier than this.

Pride inside

I used to have a name, chosen for me by another.
Time to pick and choose myself –
I'll have an LGBTTQQIAAP, please Carol.
What does that add up to? Too black to be gay, too gay to be black, be a lady they say, be a nasty woman. Be a man.
Be.

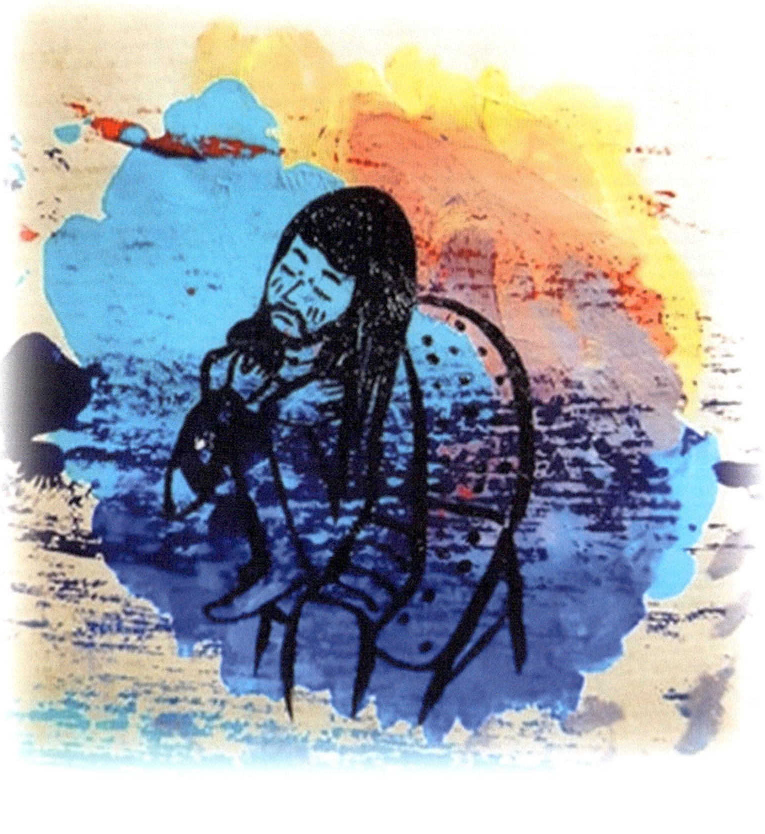

No melancholy

She used to be useless. She used to be fat. She used to giggle when a man paid her attention, a compliment or dinner. She used to feel used. Then her eyes and mouth opened wide and she took a deep breath and she screamed like a banshee, announcing her own birth.

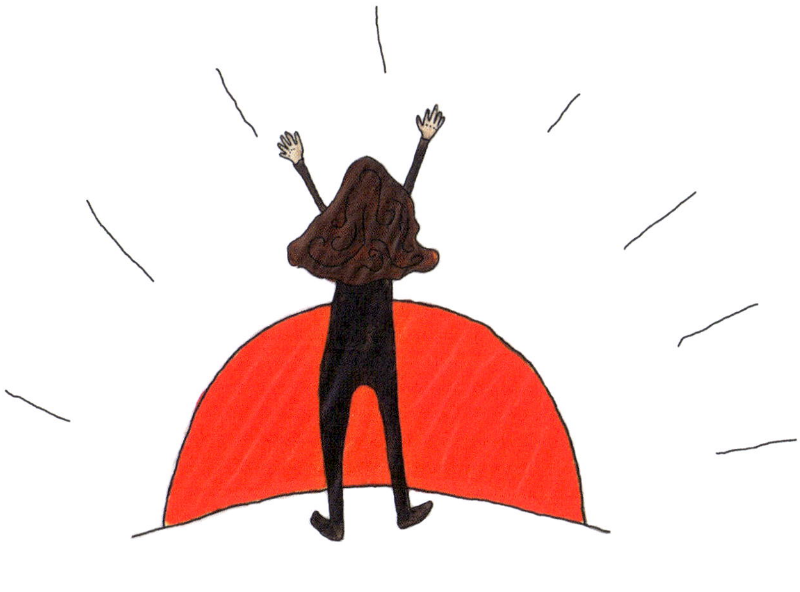

The troubles of drying laundry in the rainforest

He knew before the trip. He must expose as little skin as possible to bullet ants, poison dart frogs, wandering spiders and never wear wet clothing, while travelling light.
A sitting duck to jaguars, rattle snakes and anacondas, he stares at socks and underpants lined up in 88% humidity.
I'll miss him.

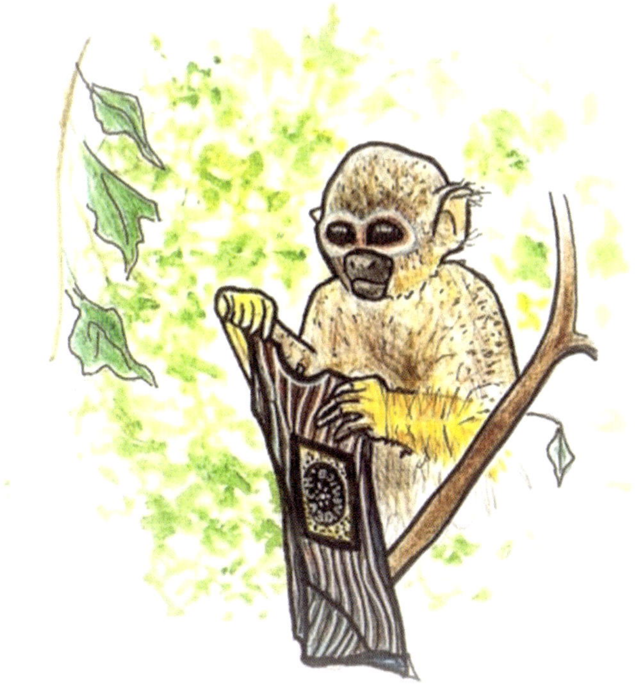

Primo Ballerino

Behind his closet doors, his spirit is allowed to shine. In his cocoon he heals from the mishandling of his je-ne-sais-quoi, until his spark ignites, incinerating all the walls. No longer he or she, they rise up from the ashes, and their wings are strong enough to shelter others, too.

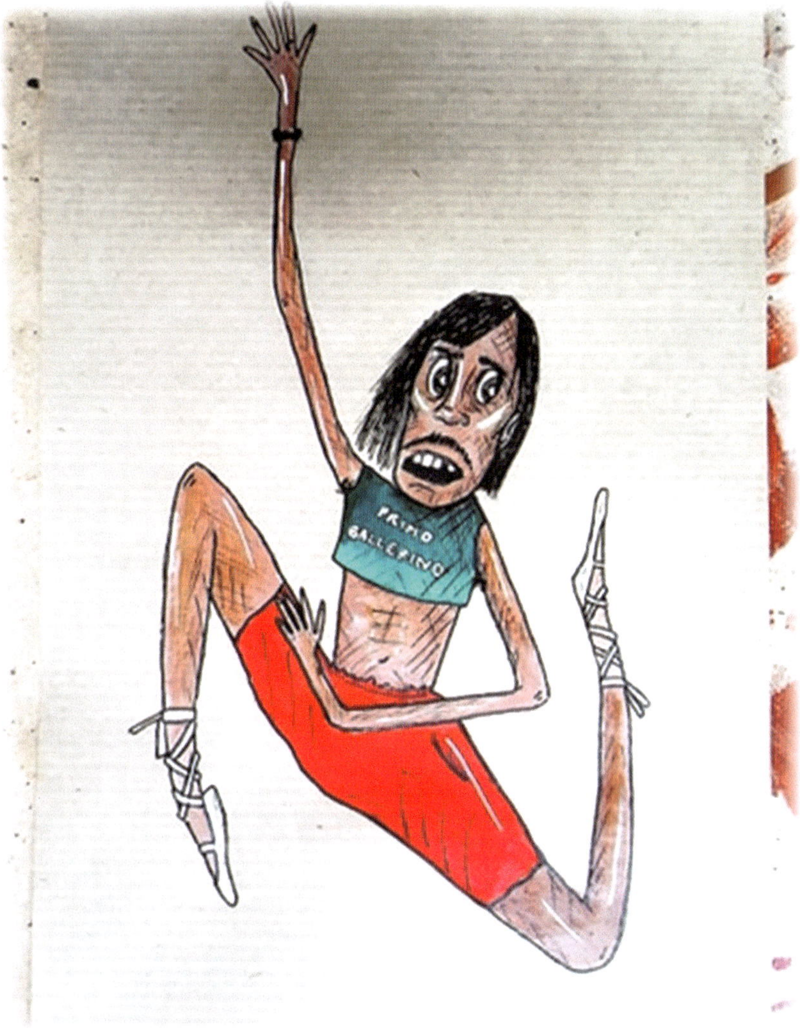
PRIMO
BALLERINO

Shooting a Star

One afternoon, uncertain of the purpose of his action, a newspaper man assassinated a star. He spotted it, took aim and fired, surprised how quickly it came tumbling down.
He watched it lie there, flackering faintly. Amidst a crowd of onlookers, applauding his success, he wished he hadn't, but to no avail.

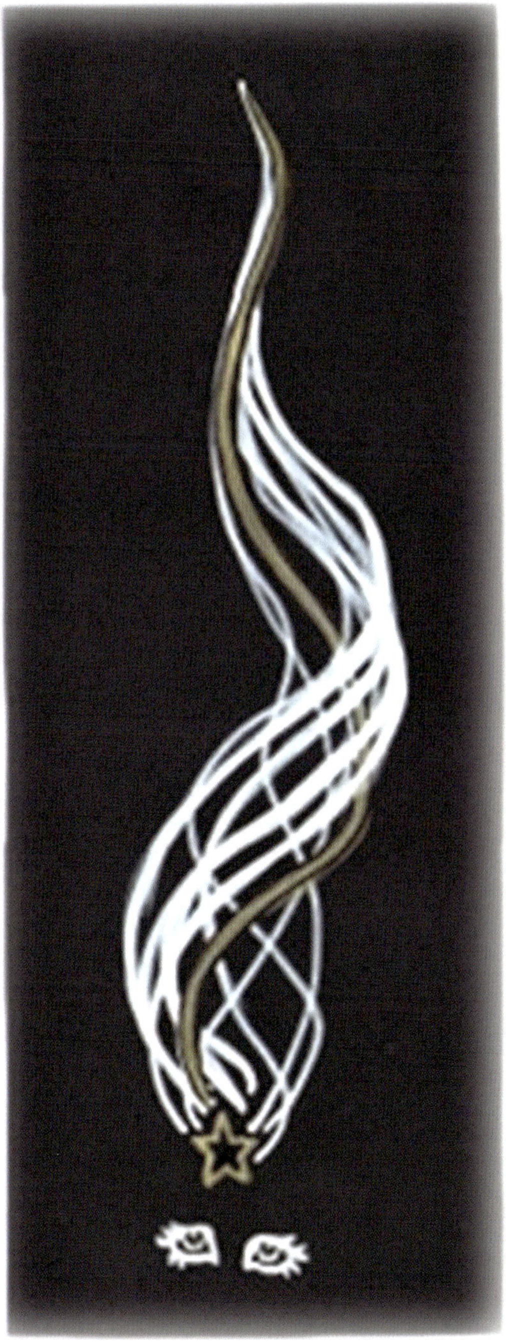

The Spider

The phone rings at 3 am. 'Please, can you come?' his mother pleads. We throw on clothes and leave. With tyres screeching for a break, we arrive, minutes later.
'A spider,' he exclaims, incredulous. 'A fucking spider!'
No, my darling, no. It's that your dad's no longer here to step on it.

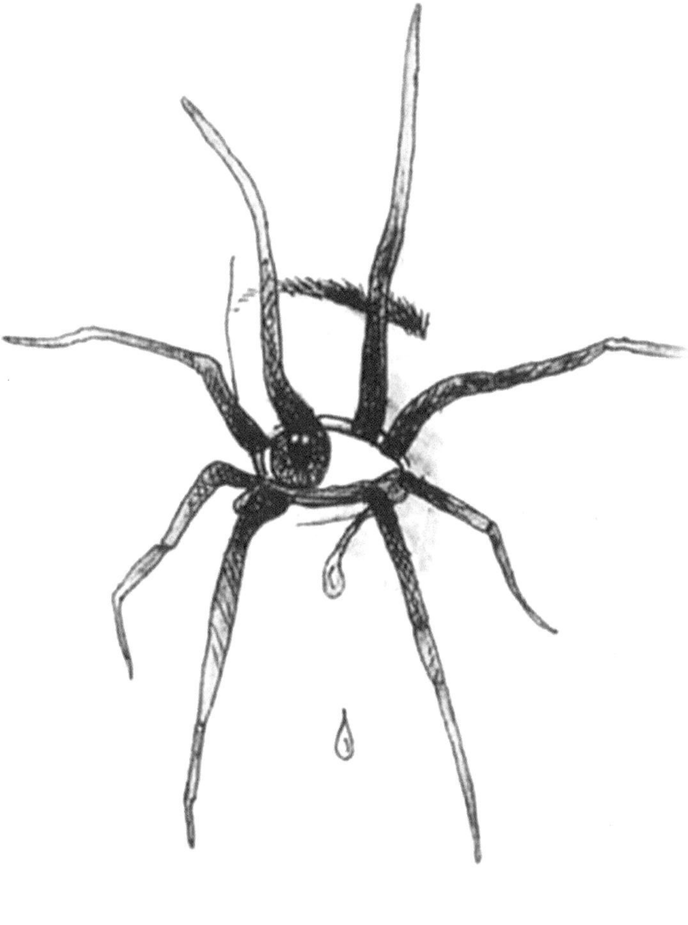

The Neighbour

'Hello,' I offer, but the ancient man does not reply. He cannot hear me speaking now, I guess. Come rain or shine, he wields his tools and perseveres in his attempt to resurrect that empty vase, that rusty caravan.
'Cobwebs are lovelier in mist,' he says, just when I turn my back.

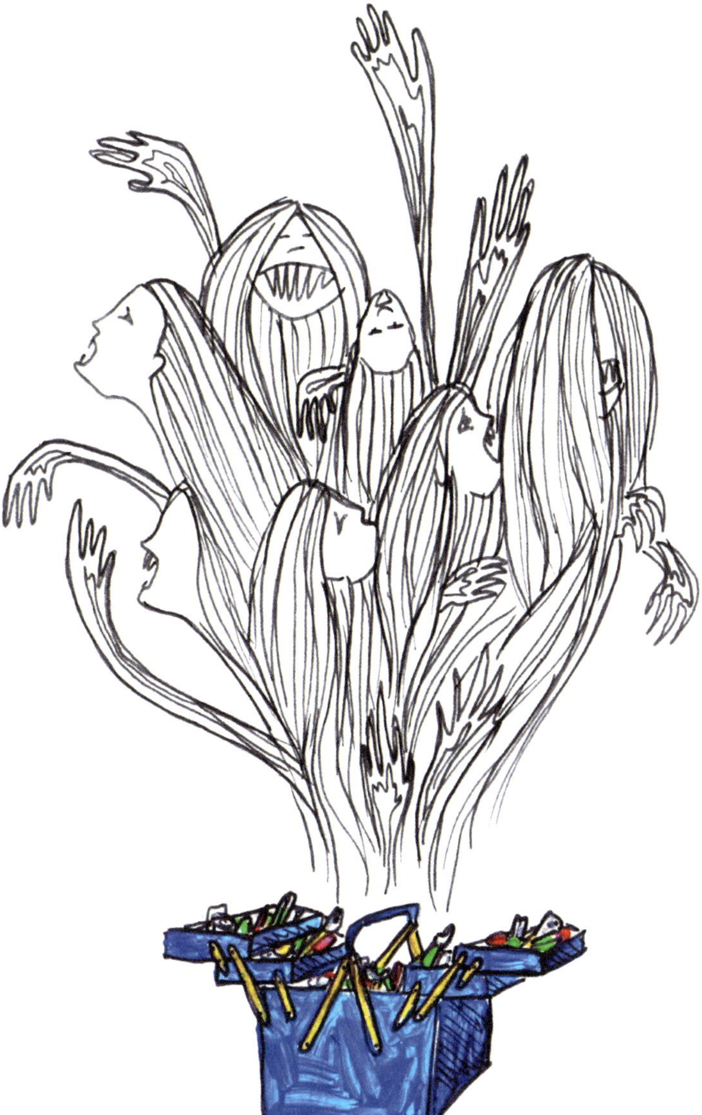

The Search

He's staring at the vortex now, the endless round and round, and longs for it to end. His friend Maheer is looking for true love, his sister Mhairie searches for perfection. But in that maelstrom of abandonment, our Daniel simply longs to find the matching socks to all his single ones.

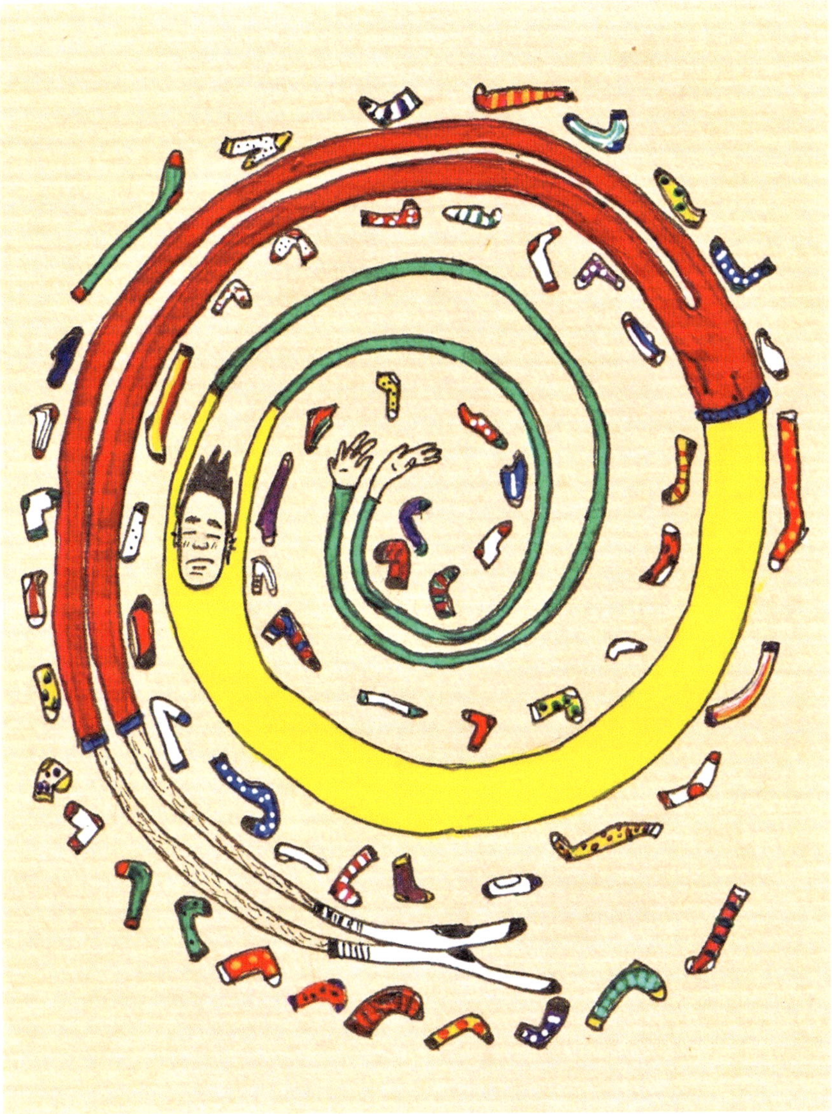

Hairy backed men

The massive silverback is close – his giant hand can stroke my skin. With deference, I breathe his scent, he smells of jungle and hot musk. Drenched in testosterone and sweat, I wake with guilt and grasp for just a strand of here and now. Instead, I feel the reassuring warmth of you.

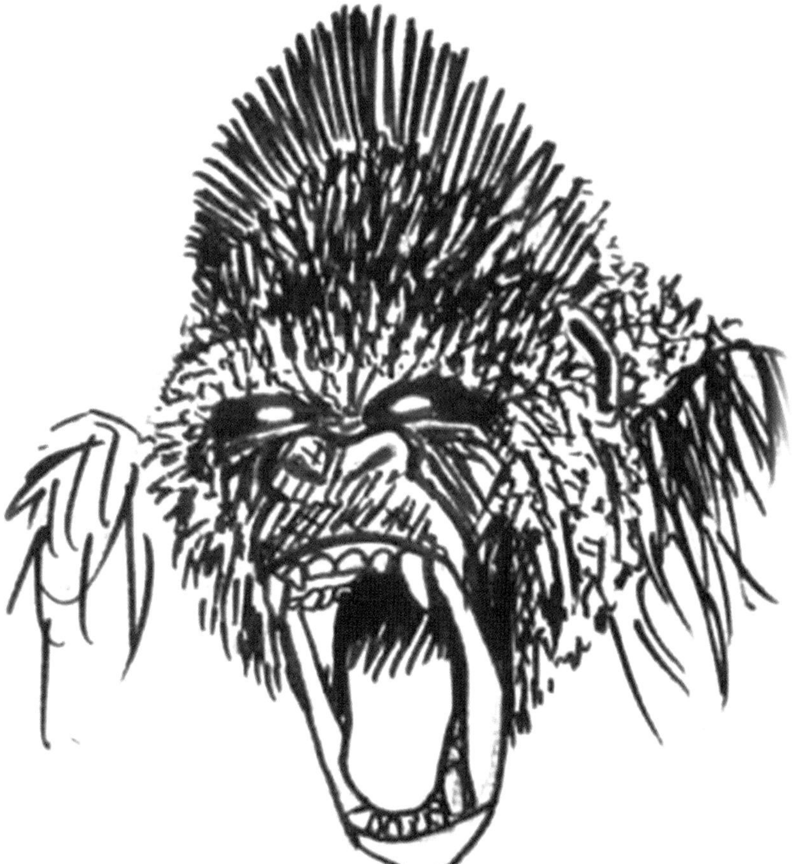

Riding on the Wild Side

The wolf pretends to be her nan, with big old eyes, all kind and frail. And yet she knows his game and calls his bluff. 'You've eaten her, you monstrous thing, take this!'
She wields her sword.
And slain, the dead imposter's in the well.
It happens when The Hood's on meth.

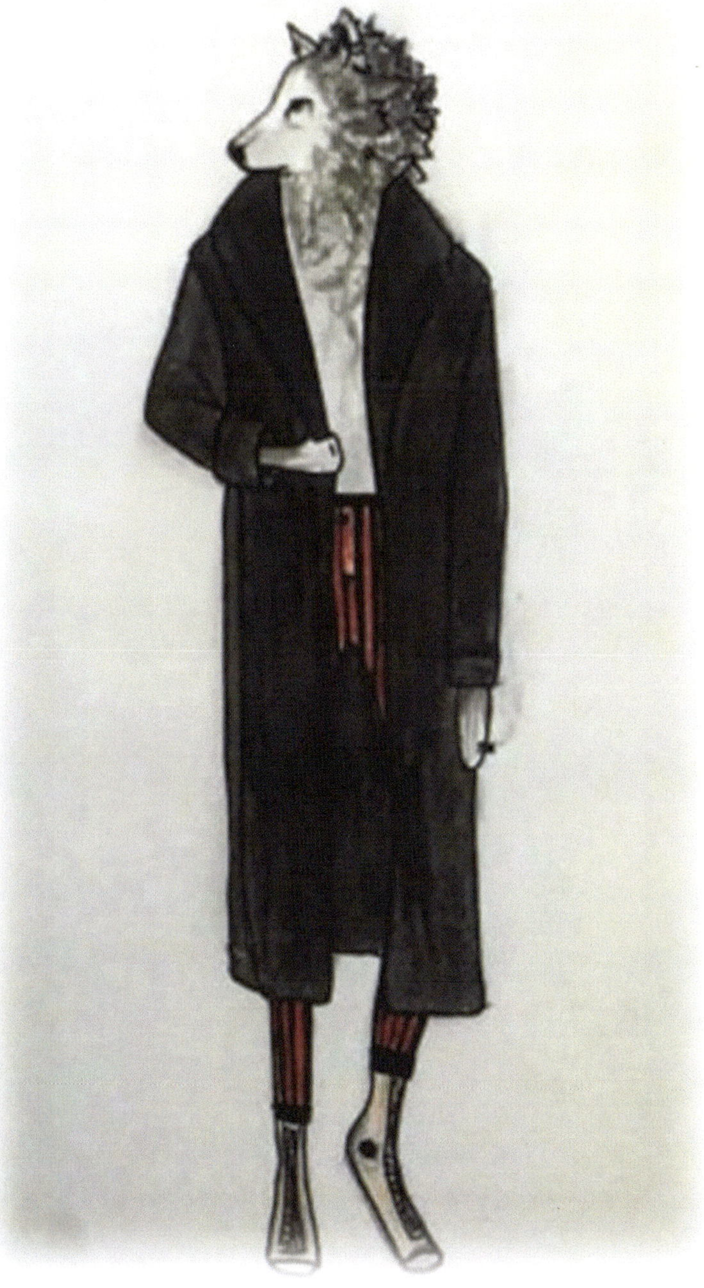